Rabbit's Gift

Gift

A FABLE FROM CHINA

TOLD BY

GEORGE SHANNON

ILLUSTRATED BY

LAURA DRONZEK

HARCOURT, INC. ▼ Orlando Austin New York San Diego Toronto London

Library of Congress Cataloging-in-Publication Data
Shannon, George.
Rabbit's gift/George Shannon; illustrated by Laura Dronzek.
p.   cm.
Summary: Woodland animals, each thinking of his neighbor, share a turnip left on their doorstep.
[1. Fables.   2. Folklore—China.]   I. Dronzek, Laura, ill.   II. Title.
PZ8.2.S43Ra   2007
398.2—dc22   2006004789
ISBN 978-0-15-206073-2

First edition
H   G   F   E   D   C   B   A

Manufactured in China

The illustrations in this book were done with acrylic paints on paper.
The display lettering was created by Georgia Deaver.
The text type was set in Bryn Mawr Book.
Color separations by Bright Arts Ltd., Hong Kong
Manufactured by South China Printing Company, Ltd., China
Production supervision by Pascha Gerlinger
Designed by Linda Lockowitz

For Sooz Appel

—G. S.

For Will and Clara

—L. D.

Rabbit twitched his nose in the cold, damp air. Time to find food. More snow was coming. Coming soon.

He hopped and pawed through the field till he found
a turnip. Then a second one, too. Quickly as he could,
Rabbit rolled them home.

Rabbit grinned as he nibbled. *A turnip always makes for a cozy meal.* Warm and safe, he thought about Donkey alone on the hill and wondered if she'd found enough to eat.

Rabbit gently butted his extra turnip to Donkey's house.
But Donkey wasn't there. Rabbit left the turnip by the door,
then hopped back home as his tracks disappeared in the
falling snow.

When Donkey returned with a potato she'd found, she nearly stepped on the turnip by the door.

"Who could have left this nice surprise?" asked Donkey. "My potato is plenty for me. Goat's always hungry. I'll take this to him."

Donkey hurried to her neighbor's. But Goat wasn't there.
Donkey left the turnip by the door, then climbed back home
as her tracks disappeared in the falling snow.

When Goat returned with a cabbage he'd found, he nearly stepped on the turnip by the door.

"Dear me," said Goat. "Someone's lost a turnip. And with all this snow! Maybe it was Deer when she passed this way?"

Goat tucked his cabbage inside the door, then rolled the turnip around the bend to Deer's house. But Deer wasn't there. Goat left the turnip by the door, then trudged back home as his tracks disappeared in the falling snow.

When Deer came home with a carrot she'd found, she nearly stepped on the turnip by the door.

"How kind," said Deer. "Someone's left me a gift. But there's no need to keep more than I can eat. With the snow this deep, Rabbit couldn't have found much food."

Deer took high steps through the deep, deep snow. Rabbit
was home, but sound asleep. Deer left the turnip by the
door, then leaped back home as her tracks disappeared
in the falling snow.

The next morning Rabbit woke up early. After a nibble of his turnip, he was ready to play. But as he stepped outside, Rabbit tripped on another turnip lying by the door.

"Who in the woods could have brought me this?" Rabbit looked for tracks, but the night's fresh snow had erased everything. "I don't know who to thank."

Then Rabbit slowly grinned. "But I know just who to share it with!"

Author's Note

Rabbit's Gift is based on a folktale that has been shared for centuries. More than twenty-five years ago, I first discovered an English translation of a German version that attributed the story to China. Since then I have found Japanese, French, and Spanish retellings. Some of those translations credit Fang Yi-K'iun, but I have not been able to trace that source. The core narrative of the story has also been collected in Syria and Jordan. No doubt, like most folktales, this story exists among and beyond these cultures. Now, through this book, I share it with you.

Chinese Symbols

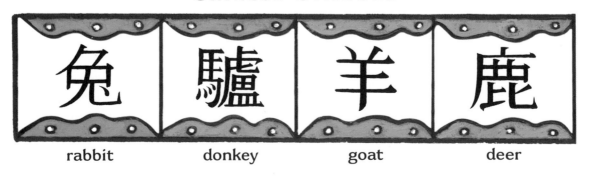

rabbit   donkey   goat   deer

"Yes, a turnip *always* makes for a cozy meal."